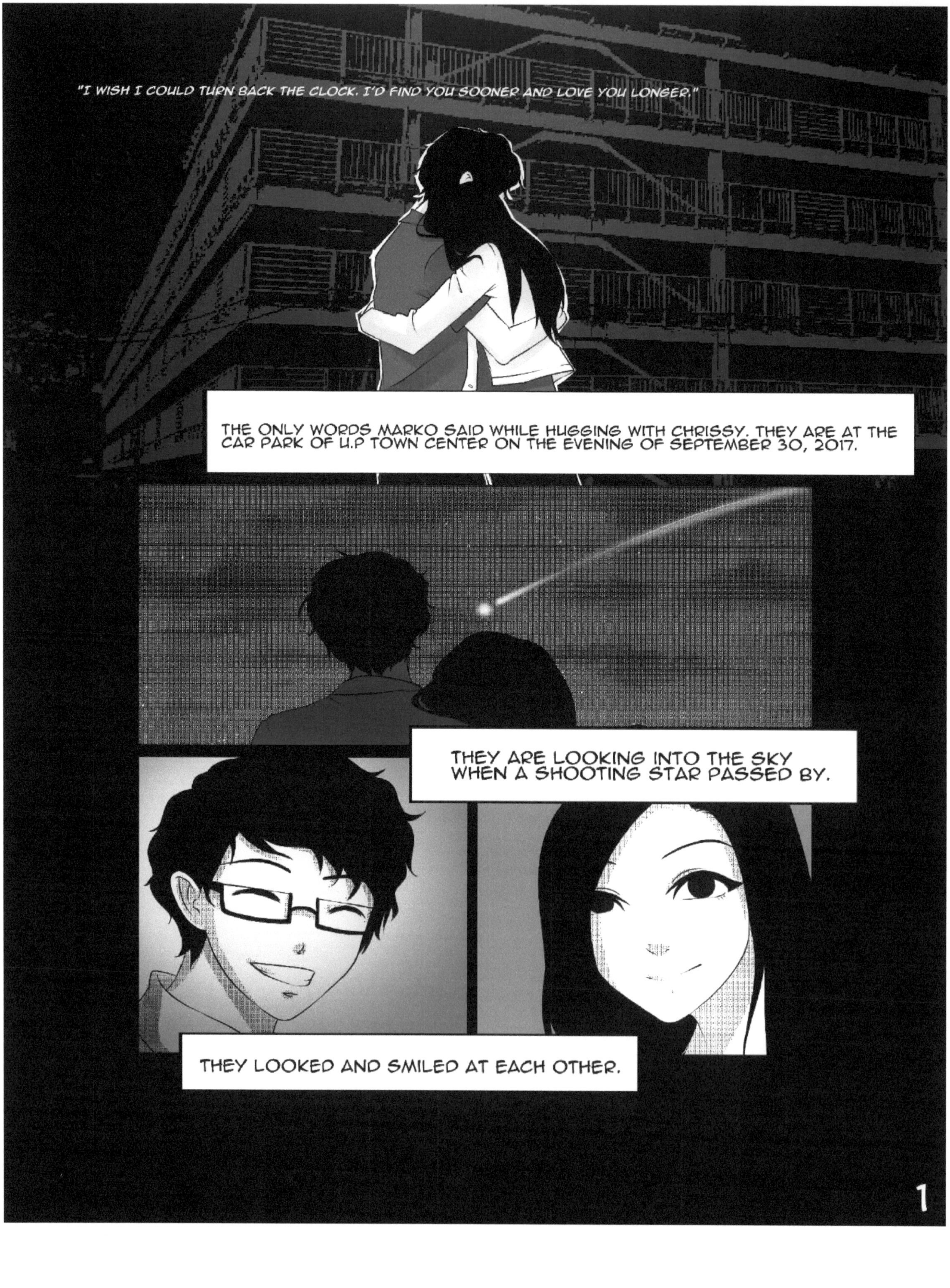

"I WISH I COULD TURN BACK THE CLOCK. I'D FIND YOU SOONER AND LOVE YOU LONGER."

THE ONLY WORDS MARKO SAID WHILE HUGGING WITH CHRISSY. THEY ARE AT THE CAR PARK OF U.P TOWN CENTER ON THE EVENING OF SEPTEMBER 30, 2017.

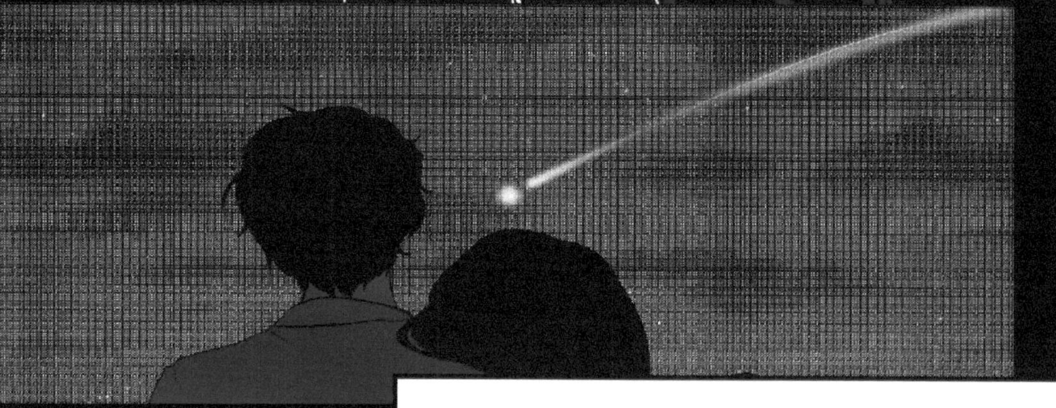

MARKO IS A WRITER WHILE CHRISSY IS A FAMOUS AMERICAN SINGER.

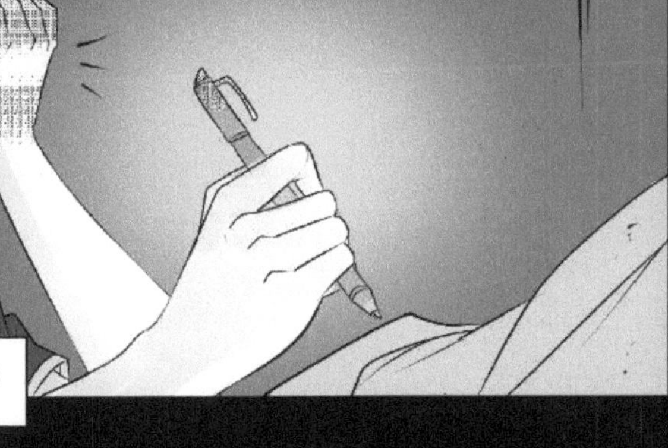

ONE DAY, MARKO WOKE UP HOLDING A MYSTERIOUS BALLPEN.
HE DIDN'T KNOW HOW IT GOT IN HIS HANDS.

HE REMEMBERED THAT HE FELL ASLEEP WHILE WRITING A LOVE LETTER.
HE IS PLANNING TO GIVE IT TO CHRISSY THE NEXT DAY.
CHRISSY TOGETHER WITH HER BAND AGAINST THE CURRENT WILL HAVE A CONCERT AT AYALA MALL SOLENAD.
WHILE MARKO WRITES HIS LOVE LETTER, HE SUDDENLY HAD A STRANGE FEELING.
"I WISH I COULD BE EVERYTHING YOU WANTED, EVERYTHING THAT YOU NEED..."

SURPRISINGLY, HE IS IN A HOSPITAL. HE IS A DOCTOR WHO IS GIVING BIRTH TO A BABY.
HE SAW THE DATE IN THE CALENDAR. IT WAS AUGUST 23, 1995.

HE WAS CONFUSED HOW HE HAD SKILLS IN GIVING BIRTH.
HE DOES NOT HAVE KNOWLEDGE IN BEING A DOCTOR.
AFTER THE OPERATION, THE BABY WAS BROUGHT TO THE NURSERY ROOM.
HE READ THE BRACELET OF THE BABY WITH THE BABY'S NAME WRITTEN, "CHRISSY COSTANZA".

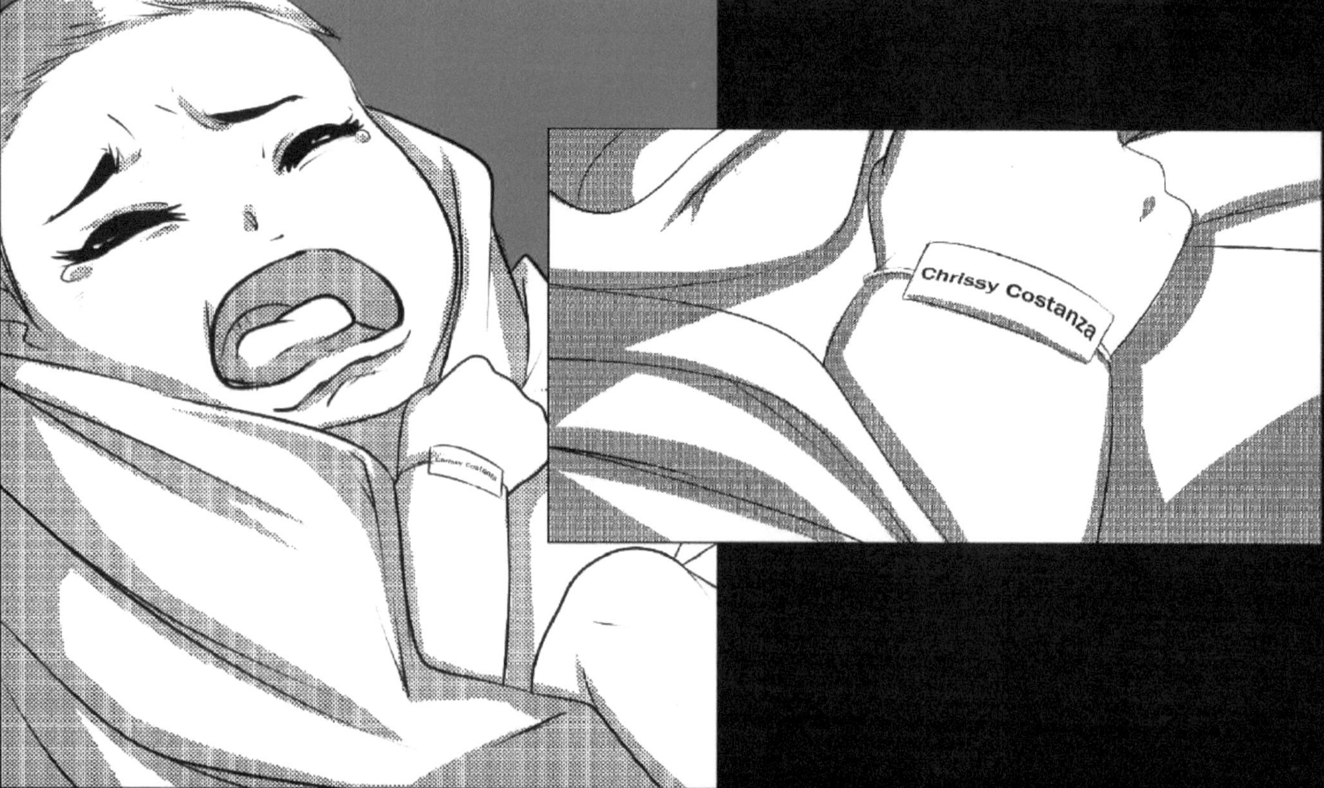

WITH A BLINK OF AN EYE, HE IS BACK AT THE PLACE AND TIME WHEN HE IS WRITING A LOVE LETTER FOR CHRISSY.
HE DISCOVERED THAT THE PEN HE USED IN WRITING WAS THE SAME REASON HE WAS ABLE TO TIME TRAVEL. HE RETURNED TO THE PAST AND SAW CHRISSY WHEN SHE WAS STILL A BABY.
HE READ AGAIN THE FIRST SENTENCE HE WROTE. "I WISH I COULD BE EVERYTHING THAT YOU WANTED..."
HE BECAME NERVOUS TO CONTINUE WRITING BECAUSE HE DID NOT KNOW WHERE HE MAY TRAVEL THIS TIME.
"I WISH I COULD BE EVERYTHING THAT YOU WANTED..."
HE THOUGHT THAT MAYBE HE SAW THE PAST BECAUSE OF THE DESIRE OF HIS HEART TO KNOW CHRISSY MORE. THE EARLIER TIME HE GOT TO KNOW HER, THE LONGER TIME HE WILL HAVE TO LOVE HER.
HE THEN QUICKLY RESEARCHED CHRISSY'S BIOGRAPHY. HE WANTED TO KEEP TRACK OF CHRISSY' LIFE AS SHE GROWS UP. HE WANTED TO TAKE CARE OF HER AND PROTECT HER.

HE WAS THERE SINCE CHRISSY WAS A BABY UNTIL SHE LEARNED TO WALK AND TO TALK.

MARKO WONDERED WHEN HE WAS NOW IN ANOTHER PLACE..
THE PLACE WAS CUTE. IT WAS FILLED WITH COLORFUL BALLOONS. THEN, HE SAW A BANNER.
WRITTEN ON IT WAS "HAPPY 1ST BIRTHDAY CHRISSY!".
Happy 1st Birthday Chrissy!
IT WAS CHRISSY'S FIRST BIRTHDAY WHEN HER PARENTS ORGANIZED A PARTY FOR HER. THEY GOT A CLOWN. THE MAN BEHIND THE CLOWN COSTUME WAS... MARKO.

HE SAW CHRISSY'S SMILE AND HEARD HER LAUGH WITH HIS FUNNY ACTS.

WHEN SHE STARTED SCHOOLING AT KINDERGARTEN, ELEMENTARY, HIGH SCHOOL, AND COLLEGE, MARKO WAS ALWAYS BY HER SIDE.
YOUNG CHRISSY WAS REALLY CHEERFUL AT SCHOOL. SHE WAS ACTIVE IN RECITATIONS SO SHE WILL ALWAYS GO HOME WITH VERY GOOD STAMPS FROM HER TEACHER MARKO.
"KIDS, WHO AMONG YOU KNOWS HOW TO WRITE YOUR NAME ALREADY?", TEACHER MARKO ASKED HIS CLASS.
"TEACHER! TEACHER! ME!", CHRISSY SHOUTED.
CHRISSY THEN WROTE HER FULL NAME IN HER NOTEBOOK AND SHOWED IT TO HER TEACHER.
Christina Nicola Costanza
"WOW! THAT'S GREAT CHRISSY. VERY GOOD. HERE'S YOUR STAR FOR TODAY.", TEACHER MARKO PRAISED HER. EVERYDAY, CHRISSY ACTIVELY PARTICIPATED IN CLASS.

THIS IS WHY SHE WAS CHOSEN BY TEACHER MARKO TO BE REWARDED AS THE "MOST OUTSTANDING STUDENT" IN THE CLASS.
CHRISSY FINISHED ELEMENTARY SCHOOL. SHE GRADUATED AT THE IMMACULATE HEART ACADEMY WITH HONORS. SHE CONTINUED HER ACADEMIC EXCELLENCE WITH THE HELP OF HER TUTOR MARKO.
SHE LIKES TO PERFORM ON STAGE DURING PROGRAMS AT HER SCHOOL.
IN HER SOPHOMORE YEAR, SHE JOINED A TALENT SHOW. SHE MET A CONTESTANT LIKE HER NAMED MARKO. THEY BECAME FRIENDS DURING THE AUDITION AND REHEARSALS EVEN IF THEY WILL BE COMPETING WITH EACH OTHER.
"CHRISSY, DO YOUR BEST! YOU CAN DO IT!" MARKO CHEERED WHEN CHRISSY WAS CALLED ON STAGE.
CHRISSY REPLIED WITH A SMILE.

SHE STARTED SINGING AND SHE CAPTURED THE HEART OF THE AUDIENCE WITH HER CHOSEN BALLAD SONG.
SINCE THEN, CHRISSY ALREADY KNEW THAT HER HEART WAS REALLY FOR MUSIC. MARKO BECAME HER MUSIC COMPANION. HE ALSO ACCOMPANIED HER ANYWHERE.
WHILE CHRISSY WAS ATTENDING COLLEGE, SHE WAS ALSO STARTING TO BUILD HER MUSIC CAREER. SHE IS COMPOSING HER SONGS, PRACTICING WITH THE BAND, AND GOING ANYWHERE FOR SOME GIGS.
DURING HER COLLEGE GRADUATION DAY, MARKO WAS THE FIRST ONE TO CONGRATULATE HER. WITH EVERY ACCOMPLISHMENT AND ACHIEVEMENT IN HER LIFE, MARKO WAS THERE TO SUPPORT HER.
CHRISSY WAS UNAWARE THAT IT WAS MARKO WHO HELPED HER ALL THE TIME. SHE DOES NOT KNOW THAT EVERY PERSON NAMED MARKO SHE MET IN HER LIFE HAS BEEN JUST ONE PERSON. SHE ALSO DOES NOT KNOW THAT MARKO SECRETLY LOVED HER FOR A LONG TIME.
CHRISSY HAD A BOYFRIEND. THEY BROKE UP. IT WAS HER FIRST HEARTBREAK. MARKO WAS THERE TO COMFORT HER.

MARKO WOKE UP AND FOUND OUT THAT EVERYTHING WAS JUST A DREAM. EVEN THE PART HE WOKE UP IN THE STORY WAS JUST A DREAM. HE THOUGHT EVERYTHING HE SAW WAS REAL. TEARS FELL DOWN FROM HIS EYES WHEN HE REALIZED NOTHING WAS REAL.
BECAUSE OF THIS, HE HAD AN IDEA WHAT TO WRITE IN HIS STORY. BEING A WRITER, HE THOUGHT THAT THROUGH WRITING THE STORY OF HIS DREAM, HE WOULD FEEL THAT THINGS BECAME TRUE.
HE WROTE THE STORY ENTITLED "DREAMING ALONE". HE WROTE THIS FICTIONAL LOVE STORY AS HIS GIFT FOR CHRISSY. MARKO GAVE IT TO CHRISSY WHEN HER BAND HAD A CONCERT AT UP TOWN CENTER.
WHEN CHRISSY READ THE WHOLE STORY, SHE QUICKLY RAN TOWARDS THE CAR PARK TO LOOK FOR THE PERSON WHO GAVE HER THE LOVE LETTER...
..SHE SAW MARKO, WHO WAS ABOUT TO LEAVE.
..SHE HUGGED HIM TIGHTLY AS THEY LOOK AT THE SKY... WATCHING THE SHOOTING STAR PASSING BY.
"THANK YOU, MARKO, FOR COMING TO MY LIFE." CHRISSY TOLD MARKO WITH A SMILE IN HER FACE.

"If a writer fell in love with you, you will never die."

For Chrissy Costanza.

"All these places I want to go don't exist without you.

All my goals come from one place. You.

You are my biggest goal. That's not wrong, is it?"

In this life, you can do what you want, you can be whatever you want to be, you can be with whoever is within your reach, you can go wherever you want to go as long as you can afford to do it. But there are things that we want that we can

never have, things that are beyond our control, beyond our capabilities, sometimes, those are the things that we want the most.. something that we think that can complete us.

In the moment we realize that not you cannot have everything you want, we give up. We lose hope.. We stop hoping, we stop moving. Without even trying if there is even a small posibility of living that dream. But for me, I think that "to dream" is one of

the things that keeps you going. Because if you have that one dream of becoming

somebody, or wanna be with somebody, That's what motivates us.. to keep improving. It's like having a purpose or a goal.

-Werdnakram

WERDNAKRAM

Mobile number: 0956-783-1178
e-mail address: iamwerdnakram@gmail.com
Werdnakram Facebook page: https://www.facebook.com/iamwerdnakram/
Werdwideweb Publishing Facebook page: https://www.facebook.com/werdwidewebpub/
Werdnakram's Laboratory Facebook page: https://www.facebook.com/werdnakramlaboratory/

ABOUT

Si Werdnakram ang author/writer ng mga sumusunod na libro at komiks:

- **Autobiography of a Sleepless Solitude Mind**
- **Reincarnation of a New Born Pride**
- **Ang Pakikipagsapalaran ni Werdnakam (Books 1 & 2)**
- **Werdnakram Chronicles**
- **Werdnakram Diaries**
- **Scientiscriptures 1&2 (Rebolusyon Laban sa Ebolusyon at Bible Mysteries)**
- **Fact You**
- **Treevia**
- **Ang Simula ng Katapusan: Pagdating at Pamumuno ng Antikristo**
- **Architects of Deception**
- **Werdnakram and the Visions of the Future**
- **Werdnakram's Guide to Pinoy Urban Legends**
- **Werdnakram's Guide to Mysteries of the Universe**

ACADEMIC BACKGROUND

1. Si Werdnakram ay nag-aral sa Bagong Silangan Elementary & High School.
2. Naka-graduate siya sa Polytechnic University of the Philippines sa kursong BS Physics.
3. Siya ay nag-OJT sa UP NISMED bilang trainee assistant & researcher.

ACHIEVEMENTS

1. Si Werdnakram ay nakapasa na sa Civil Service Professional exam
2. Siya ay nakapag-published na ng libro na Ang Pakikipagsapalaran ni Werdnakram (Book I) sa Koala Publishing House.

WRITING EXPERIENCES

1. *Nagsimula siyang nagsulat ng dyaryo noong High School na "A Monthly Dose of Dyok: Unofficially Newsmagazine of Zekhatorrs"*
2. *Ipinagpatuloy niya ang pagsusulat ng dyaryo noong college na "Quanta: Unofficial Newsmagazine of Physics Society"*
3. *Si Werdnakram ay nagsusulat blogs sa The Mark Theory webpage.*
4. *Siya ay nakapag-contribute at nagsulat ng articles sa WikiPilipinas.*
5. *Siya ay naging contributor din sa foreign online news blog na The Vincent Times.*

ISBN:
Hardbound-978-621-470-564-1
MOBI/KINDLE-978-621-470-565-8
Softbound/Paperback-978-621-470-566-5

Published by:
Poetry Planet Book Publishing House
Rosario, Pozorrubio, Pangasinan, Philippines
Contact Number: 09554960094
Email: maritesritumalta@gmail.com

POETRY PLANET
BOOK PUBLISHING HOUSE
CERTIFICATE
OF PUBLICATION
PROUDLY PRESENTED TO
Published Author
Book Title
ISBN:
Powered by:
PAMBANSANG AKLATAN NG PILIPINAS
Dreaming Alone
Written by:
MARK ANDREW B. MANAO
Illustration by:
Nicole Torio

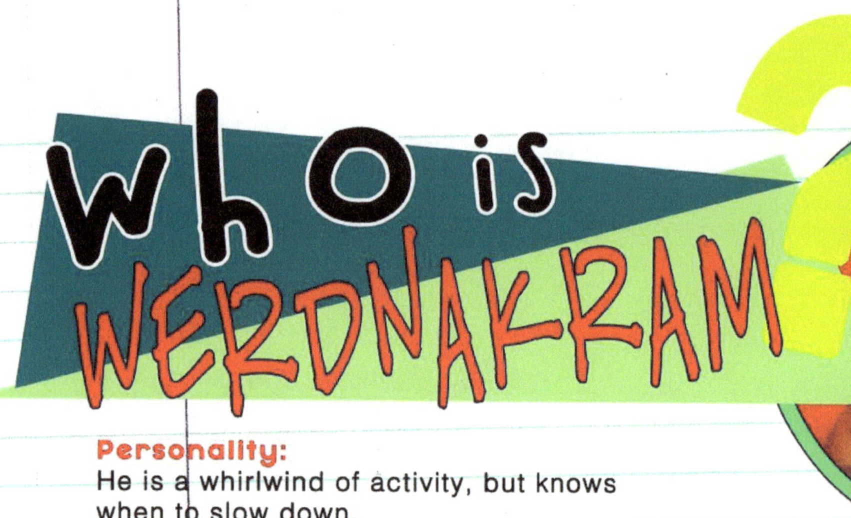

Personality:
He is a whirlwind of activity, but knows when to slow down.
One who is unyielding and hates to lose.
Highly intelligent, although he doesn't appear to be.
Able to solve difficult problems.
Value the few friends he has.
Firmly stick to his decisions until proven to be 100% wrong.

Education:
He studied BS Physics at Polytechnic University of the Philippines.

Affiliation:
Founder of Markinyourheart Foundation
Member of Physics Society

Training Experience:
Did OJT at UP National Institute of Science & Mathematics Education (NISMED)

Job Experience:
-Science Teacher at Cambridge Christian School & Imelda Operio Learning School
-Copy editor at American Institute of Physics
-Textbook Editorial Assistant at Vibal Group
-Writer/Contributor at WikiPilipinas
-Blogger at The Mark Theory
-Online Science News writer at The Vincent Times

Hobbies:
Band Vocalist
Basketball
Playing Billiards
Arcade games
Traveling

Food:
Graham cake
Leche flan
Chocolates
Yoghurt
Migoreng noodles

Genre:
SciFi
Time travel
Action

Movies:
Time Traveler's Wife
Time Machine
Looper
Artificial Intelligence
Back to the Future
Windstruck
The Notebook
Bubble Boy
The Girl Next Door

Series:
Doctor Who
Game of Thrones
Timeless
12 Monkeys
The Big Bang Theory
Fringe
Chuck

Anime:
Great Teacher Onizuka
Assassination Classroom
Kuoko's Basketball
Death Note
Tokyo Ghoul
Parasyte

Music:
Grunge
Metalcore
Alternative Rock
Metalcore
Post-hardcore

Actor:
Jason Statham
Brad Pitt
Hugh Jackman

Actress:
Kristin Kreuk
Elisha Cuthbert
Rachel McAdams

Dream Girl:

Chrissy Costanza

www.ingramcontent.com/pod-product-compliance
Lightning Source LLC
LaVergne TN
LVHW071116160826
845679LV00004B/1100
9786214705665